From Best Friend To Bully

TANYA SAVORY

FROM BEST FRIEND TO BULLY

TP THE TOWNSEND LIBRARY

For more titles in the Townsend Library,
visit our website: **www.townsendpress.com**

Townsend Press, Inc.
439 Kelley Drive
West Berlin, New Jersey 08091
cs@townsendpress.com

ISBN-13: 978-1-59194-272-6
ISBN-10: 1-59194-272-1

Library of Congress Control Number:
2011941468

Chapter 1

Pam and Emily had been best friends since before they could remember. Emily even had a picture of the two of them side by side in baby strollers. Every time they looked at that picture, they burst out laughing.

"You hardly have any hair on your head," Emily would snort between giggles.

"Well, look at you!" Pam would snicker. "You're sucking your thumb!"

The two girls had always loved joking

with each other and poking fun at things they thought were funny about each other. But they had never been mean or hurtful. The kidding never went too far. However, for some reason, things had begun to change recently. More than once, Pam made jokes that really hurt Emily's feelings.

"Oh, wow," Pam had said right after Christmas. "That new sweater your mom gave you looks like something my grandmother would wear."

When Emily frowned and just walked away, Pam called after her.

"Hey, I'm just kidding! Can't you take a joke?"

Later that day Pam sneaked Emily a note in class telling her that she was sorry.

After school, she invited Emily over to her house to play.

Sometimes friends make mistakes, Emily wrote in her diary the next day. *But best friends stay best friends.*

However, as time went on, Pam made mean jokes more and more often. And her apologies came less and less often. Sometimes Emily wasn't sure if they *were* best friends anymore. Finally, something happened near the middle of the school year that made Emily wonder if they were even friends at all.

It all began when Mr. Benson, their teacher, announced that his 4th-grade class was going to put on a play for the whole school later in the year. There would be acting, music, and singing in the play. There would be fun costumes and beautiful sets.

"Everyone has to be involved," Mr. Benson said. "If you don't want to be in the play, you can help with something else."

Most of the students wanted a part. And when Mr. Benson explained that the starring role was a girl's part and that it involved singing a lot of fun songs, nearly half the girls in the class wanted the starring role. Several girls raised their hands excitedly and said they wanted that part.

"Here's the thing," Mr. Benson explained. "It's not as easy as just volunteering. You'll have to try out for the part you want."

Pam raised her hand.

"You mean like whoever is the best gets the best part?" she asked.

"That's right," Mr. Benson said. "So you'll really need to practice the part you want. The harder you work, the better chance you'll have."

On the way home from school that afternoon on the bus, Pam talked nonstop. She was very excited about the play. And she was certain that she would get the best role.

"A star! I'm going to be a star," Pam said. "I love to sing. No one can beat me at that!"

Emily smiled at her friend. Pam had always been a bit of a show-off. She liked attention. Emily was pretty sure Pam's great singing would get her the starring role in the play. Even so . . .

"Hey, I think I'll try out too," Emily said.

Pam got a funny look on her face. "Really? For the starring role? Why?"

Emily acted like it was no big deal.

"I don't know. It would be fun. We could practice together and stuff."

Pam still looked unsure, but she just shrugged.

"Okay. Whatever. But you can't really sing very well, you know."

Emily didn't argue. She knew Pam was right. Maybe she couldn't sing as well as Pam, but that didn't mean she couldn't try out. After all, there was acting too, not just singing.

"I can try my best, anyway," Emily said.

For the next two weeks, Emily and Pam got together after school nearly every day and practiced. Well, Emily practiced. Pam wasn't really interested in rehearsing the lines for the play. Mostly, she just danced around and sang the songs into a mirror. While Emily rehearsed lines, Pam tried to figure out how she'd wear her hair in the play.

Finally, it was tryout day.

No one even came close to singing as well as Pam.

But Emily was the best actress.

Mr. Benson and two other teachers

watched quietly, but they clapped loudly for each student. It was impossible to tell which students would get which parts.

"Friday morning, I'll post a list," Mr. Benson announced. "It will show everyone's part or job in the play. It won't be easy to choose! All of you have done a great job."

Chapter 2

That night, it was hard for Emily to sleep. She'd never admitted it to anyone, but she secretly hoped she'd get the part. Emily tossed and turned. Finally, around midnight, she picked up her diary and wrote down her hidden feelings.

Okay, I'll be really happy for Pam if she gets this part. But I have to be honest. I would be so excited if Mr. Benson picked me!! Anyway, I'm sure Pam would be happy for me too. She could really help me a lot with singing. Oh well. I'm just going to have to wait until the morning. I don't know if I'll be able to sleep at all tonight!

When Pam and Emily walked into their classroom the next morning, a group of students was gathered around a long piece of paper posted on the bulletin board. It was the list!

"All right!"

"Oh, man. That's totally not the part I wanted."

"I'll be happy with whatever I get."

Pam and Emily's classmates' responded noisily to the list. But everyone turned to stare at the two girls when they entered the room.

"You got it!" Allison said excitedly.

"Look! Look!" Nina shouted, pointing to the list.

Pam rushed over to the bulletin board with a squeal. Then her smile faded. It was not her name at the top of the list—it was Emily's. In fact, Pam had been given only a small part. For a moment she looked like she might cry. Then she looked angrily at her best friend.

"Whatever. I don't care," Pam said. "This play is stupid anyway."

Then she walked right past Emily without even speaking to her.

"Shh! Here she comes!"

When Emily entered the cafeteria for lunch the following Monday, Pam was laughing with Jen, Allison, and Nina. They'd all had their heads together like they were telling secrets. But as soon as Jen saw Emily, she warned the other girls, and they all stopped talking.

"What were you all talking about?" Emily asked with a smile. She wondered if she had missed a good story or something.

Jen, Allison, and Nina were silent. But Pam sighed and looked annoyed.

"Nothing *you* need to know about," Pam said. Then she glanced at the other girls and grinned.

Suddenly, Emily wasn't hungry. For some reason, Pam hadn't called Emily back over the weekend about getting together like they always did on Saturday. Emily had just figured that Pam was still upset about the play. Sometimes Pam pouted like that when she didn't get her way. She always got over it after a day or two.

But this was different. Pam had barely looked at Emily this morning in class. And now she was acting even weirder.

The five girls sat in silence for a few minutes. Allison and Nina looked nervous, but Jen kept looking at Pam and giggling.

"Hey," Pam finally said. "Does anyone know if Mr. Benson has a cat or dog at his home?"

Jen snickered. "I don't think he has either," she said, holding back a laugh.

"Oh, that's right," Pam said loudly, looking right at Emily. "That's because

THE TEACHER'S PET IS AT OUR SCHOOL!"

The table exploded with laughter. Some other kids sitting nearby joined in, giggling and staring at Emily.

"Yeah! Teacher's pet!" shouted a student that Emily didn't even know. "But she's not a bird, because she sure can't sing!"

For a second, Emily felt like she might be sick. Was Pam making a joke about *her* in front of everyone? Why would she do that? Emily thought that maybe she just didn't understand.

"I don't get it," Emily said quietly, looking at Pam. "What are you talking about?"

"Oh, right," Pam said and rolled her

eyes. "Like you don't know you're the teacher's pet. How else do you think you got that part in the play? Mr. Benson only gave it to you because you make good grades. Everyone knows you can't sing—even Mr. Benson."

Emily was too surprised and hurt to even speak. It felt like the entire cafeteria was staring at her now. Emily could feel her cheeks burning. Even though she fought it, her eyes were filling up with tears.

"She's gonna cry! Crybaby!" A shout came from someone down the table.

"Come on, Emily," Nina said quietly, sounding a little worried. "Pam's just joking around. It's no big deal."

Emily hid her face by pretending to

be interested in her lunch. Pam turned her back on Emily and began giggling about something else with Jen. Before long, everyone went back to eating lunch. Everyone forgot about it.

Everyone but Emily.

For the rest of the day, Emily barely spoke to anyone. She didn't raise her hand to answer questions like she usually did. She didn't laugh at Mr. Benson's corny jokes. And when the final bell rang, Emily rushed to gather her things and get out of the classroom. She sat alone in a seat near the back of the bus.

Did I really only get this part because I make good grades? Emily wondered. *Does everyone think I can't sing?*

Chapter 3

"What's the matter? Don't you feel well?" Emily's mother asked her that evening. Emily had barely eaten any of her dinner.

"I'm okay. Just tired, I guess," Emily said.

"You'd better get some extra rest tonight then," her mother replied. "Your days are going to start getting longer with play rehearsal after school."

Emily just sighed. "Yeah."

Her mother looked at her. "You don't sound very excited about it. I thought you couldn't wait to start rehearsing with all your friends."

Emily tried to smile. She didn't really want to talk about Pam. "I'm excited. I guess I'm just . . . maybe . . . a little nervous."

At this point, Emily's older brother, Robert, looked up from shoveling in mashed potatoes.

"Nervous? What's there to be nervous about?"

Robert was 16, and he played guitar. More than anything, he loved to perform for friends and even strangers. He never seemed nervous.

"It's different for you," Emily said with a frown. "You don't have to sing."

"That's the truth," Robert said with a laugh. "If I sang, everyone would run away screaming."

When Robert saw his sister's worried face, he quickly said, "But that's me, not you. I've heard you singing in your room. You sound pretty good."

"Yeah, but that's in my room," Emily said. "What if I get scared in front of an audience? They'll all laugh at me."

"Hey, just picture them all sitting there in their underwear," Robert said with a grin. "Then there's no way you can be nervous."

Emily giggled and began eating.

"Well," her mother said, "Whether you imagine people in their underwear or not, you'll do great. I know it. And you should know it too. You got that part because of all your hard work."

"Do you really think so?" Emily asked hopefully.

Her mother looked surprised. "Well of course I think so. I know so."

Emily went to sleep that night hoping things would be different the next day. After all, she and Pam were best friends, right? Pam would probably pass her an apology note in the morning, and everything would be okay. And Nina had said they were all just kidding, hadn't she?

Maybe it was all a joke, Emily wrote in

her diary just before turning off the light.

I didn't think it was very funny. But maybe I'm too sensitive. Pam always says I am. Tomorrow will be a better day.

But Tuesday wasn't one bit better. Pam made it very clear that she was hanging out with other friends. And Emily wasn't invited. Making matters worse, everyone in Emily's class knew something was up between Pam and Emily. Emily felt like she had twenty-five sets of eyes on her all the time.

At lunch, Emily decided to sit alone rather than risk being laughed at again. She ate quickly with her head down. When she stood up to leave, she saw Nina looking at her from across the cafeteria. Nina looked a little uncomfortable, but she didn't wave back when Emily waved at her.

Emily asked for permission to return to her classroom early. Mr. Benson allowed his students to read or work quietly for the last 15 minutes of lunch if they didn't want to stay in the cafeteria. It was usually the shy kids or the kids without friends who chose to return early.

"That's crazy," Pam always said. "Only a loser would *want* to go back to the classroom early."

Emily had always agreed. But now here she was, walking through the door 15 minutes early. Mr. Benson looked surprised when he saw her, but he just smiled and nodded.

Emily sat down and took a quick look around. There was Tony, the new boy who stuttered when he talked. There was Kara, the girl who hardly ever spoke to anyone. And there was Annie, the girl who got picked on because her clothes looked old and funny. Emily had always thought of these students as the kids who didn't belong. Actually, she'd never thought much about them at all. Mostly, she'd ignored them. Now she was surprised when Annie gave her a little wave from across the room.

The end of the day could not come soon enough for Emily. She grabbed her things and prepared to rush out the door again. But as Emily passed Mr. Benson's desk, he motioned for her to come over.

"So, are you ready for play practice tomorrow after school?" Mr. Benson asked. "You're our star, you know," he added with a kind smile.

"I guess so," Emily said quickly. She wouldn't look at Mr. Benson.

"You know, Emily," Mr. Benson said quietly, "if something's bothering you, or if you're worried about the play, you can talk to me. I'm all ears."

After saying this, Mr. Benson pointed to his very large ears and grinned. Usually, this would have made Emily laugh. Today, it didn't.

"I know, Mr. Benson," Emily said. "But I have to go."

Emily dashed out to get a seat in the

back of the bus. Sitting across from her was Annie. She was wearing a pair of jeans that looked like boy's pants. And her shirt had a small hole in it on the left shoulder. But she looked at Emily and smiled.

"It sure is bouncy back here, isn't it?" Annie said. "You want a piece of gum?"

It was the first time Annie had ever spoken to Emily. Emily was surprised at how friendly she seemed. Only a few days ago, Emily would not have thought about talking to Annie. She might have even worried about what other students thought. But now she didn't really care. It was just nice to see a friendly smile.

"Yeah, thanks," Emily said, taking the gum. "It's crazy back here."

"You've got that big part in the play, don't you?" Annie asked shyly. "You must be brave. There's no way I could do that. I'm helping with costumes instead."

At that moment, Pam and Jen got on the bus. Pam looked back at Emily talking to Annie. Then she said something to Jen while pointing toward the back of the bus, and both girls laughed loudly.

Emily sighed. "Sometimes I don't feel so brave," she admitted to Annie.

Chapter 4

That night after dinner, Emily decided to tell her mom what was going on. Her mother listened quietly until Emily was finished.

"You and Pam have been friends for a long time," Emily's mom finally said. "Maybe when you start working on the play together, she'll stop acting this way. You've told me that sometimes she says mean things and then apologizes later."

"But what if she doesn't apologize? What if nothing changes?" Emily asked.

"Well, we'll figure something out if and when that happens," her mother said. "But I'm hopeful that Pam will remember what a good friend you are."

Emily was hopeful too. However, the next day all her hopes disappeared. Pam continued to either ignore Emily or giggle with Jen, Allison, and Nina. And when it came time for play practice after school, things only got worse.

"Pam, would you and Jen *please* stop talking!" Mr. Benson asked for the second time. Every time Emily started to practice her lines, the two girls chattered loudly. When she tried to sing, Pam rolled her eyes and snickered. In between, Pam spent her time whispering to some of the other girls in the play and pointing at Emily.

When Mr. Benson had to ask Pam to be quiet for the third time, he had had enough.

"Pam, perhaps you'd like to tell everyone what is so interesting that you have to talk about it all through rehearsal," he said.

"It's nothing," Pam said. "We were just . . . " She looked at Jen and giggled. "We were just talking about our pets."

Several girls burst out laughing. Mr. Benson just sighed and shook his head. It didn't make much sense to him.

"Okay, enough! We're here to practice

this play, not chat about our pets."

At this, there was another outburst of laughter. Emily's face turned red. Even when the girls finally quieted down, Emily felt sick and dizzy. She couldn't remember her lines. Her throat felt tight. When she sang, she thought she sounded like a chicken squawking.

Emily rushed out of the school at the end of practice and stood alone waiting for Robert to pick her up. He had just gotten his driver's license, and she didn't blame him for taking his time driving over to the school. But she really wished he had been there when she came out. She didn't want to deal with Pam and the other girls anymore.

"Hey, Emily."

Emily jumped. She hadn't even seen Nina walking over to her.

"What do you want?" Emily said angrily, not even looking at Nina.

Nina was looking around nervously. When she heard voices and laughter coming from the school entrance, she spoke quickly.

"I just wanted to say that I'm glad you got that part . . . and . . . and . . . "

"And *what*?" Emily asked. "And you think I'm the teacher's pet?"

"No!" Nina said, looking sad. "I meant to tell you that I think Pam's being mean. I don't really think it's funny. That's all."

Now Emily turned and stared at Nina.

"Then why do you laugh when she

makes fun of me?"

"I'm sorry. I won't anymore," Nina said in a rush. "It's just that Pam says she doesn't want me to be friends with you."

At that moment, Robert pulled up. He honked the horn loudly so that everyone would see he was driving. He had the radio blasting.

"Well, I have to go," was all Emily said. She got in the car and slammed the door loudly.

"What's wrong with you?" Robert shouted over the music, looking at his little sister. When he saw tears in her eyes, he turned off the music.

"Hey . . . seriously. What's the matter?"

Emily told her brother everything from

beginning to end. She even included things she hadn't told her mother, like how Pam made fun of her in the cafeteria in front of everyone. She finished by telling Robert that now Pam was trying to keep other girls from being friends with her. By the time she was done, they were back home sitting in the driveway. Robert just turned off the car and shook his head.

"Whoa. It sounds like your best friend is a bully. And, believe me, that sure is something I know about."

"What do you mean?" Emily asked, looking at Robert closely. "What do you know about bullies?"

"Well, back a few years ago, there were some boys in my class that used to pick on me. They'd call me names and hit me sometimes."

"*You?* They picked on you?" Emily asked in surprise. She'd always thought everyone liked her brother. He was popular, funny, and even played guitar in a band.

"Yeah. They thought I was a sissy because I liked the guitar better than football."

"That's stupid," Emily said. "So what did you do? Did you hit them back?"

"No," Robert said. "That's the thing about bullies. They want to upset you. Upsetting you makes them feel stronger. So they want you to hit back or cry or run away. But sometimes, if you ignore them, they lose interest in picking on you. Then again, sometimes you have to face them and tell them to stop. It depends on the bully, I guess."

Then Robert explained that he had told a teacher about the bullies. The teacher spoke to the two boys that had been bothering Robert. She also told Robert to do his best to ignore the bullies and to stay close to his friends at recess and in the cafeteria.

"They still picked on me for a while," Robert explained. "It's not like bullies just disappear. But when they finally figured out that they couldn't upset me, it wasn't as much fun for them."

Emily thought about this for a while. Then she sighed.

"But it *does* upset me," she said. "It's different, because Pam was my friend. My *best* friend."

"Yeah, that's hard," Robert agreed. They sat in silence for a while. Then Robert came up with an idea.

"Maybe you should just ask her why she's acting this way. And maybe tell her how you feel."

"It makes me scared to even think of doing that," Emily said. "She's being so mean to me."

Robert nodded and agreed that it wouldn't be easy.

"How about this," Robert said. "Practice what you want to say—just like you practiced for the play. Just like I practice the guitar. When you're sure of what you're going to say, it won't seem so hard or so scary. You know why I'm not nervous when I play? It's because I know I'm ready."

"If I talk to Pam, do you think she'll she stop being a bully? Will we be friends again?" Emily asked.

"I don't know," her brother said honestly. "Sometimes friends change. But you need to stand up for yourself. Like I said, sometimes the best way to deal with a bully is to let her know that you're not afraid to face her."

Chapter 5

That night, Emily wrote in her diary exactly what she wanted to say to Pam. She read it over and over. She spoke it out loud like she had done with her lines in the play. She even rehearsed it for her cat. Emily was a little nervous when she went to bed, but she wasn't afraid. She knew what she was going to say. She knew she wouldn't mess it up.

"Pam, wait!" Emily said the next morning as they were headed to their classroom from the bus. "I need to talk to you."

Pam looked surprised and just a little scared.

"About what?" she asked, not looking at Emily. "The bell's going to ring."

Emily took a deep breath. She could feel her heart racing.

"I just wanted to say that I know you're mad about the play. I know you wanted the part that I got. But we've been friends forever, and I don't understand why you're treating me like this. It hurts my feelings when you make fun of me in front of everyone."

Pam didn't say anything for a few seconds. Then she sighed and said, "Is that all? Because the bell's going to ring."

Emily nodded. "I just wanted you to know that."

Then Pam saw Jen walking toward her and waved. She looked at Emily and rolled her eyes. "You are *so* super-sensitive about everything!" she said loudly. "Whatever."

For the rest of that day, Pam continued ignoring Emily. But now Emily didn't feel quite as bad about it. She had said what she needed to say. Now it was up to Pam to say she was sorry.

At lunch, Emily sat with Annie. They talked about the play, Mr. Benson's crazy jokes, and food they hated. Emily had to laugh when Annie described how she had eaten an entire jar of peanut butter last year and had been sick for two whole days.

"It's not really my favorite food anymore," Annie said with a grin.

It was the first time in a long time that Annie did not go back to the classroom early. And it was the first time that week that Emily wasn't totally upset about Pam. Emily saw Pam looking at her from across the cafeteria. Pam leaned in and said something to Jen, and they both laughed. It still hurt, but maybe not quite so much.

That afternoon during play practice, Emily tried to focus on her part. It wasn't easy. Pam talked and giggled. Once, while Emily was singing, Pam put her fingers in her ears and made a face when Mr. Benson wasn't looking. This time, however, Emily just closed her eyes and kept on singing. She thought about what both her mother and Mr. Benson had said.

You got this part because of all your hard work.

You're our star!

When she finished, everyone except Pam and Jen clapped. Some of the boys working on painting the sets even came over to clap for Emily.

"Wow, that was good," Tony said.

Then Nina came over. Pam was frowning at her, but Nina just kept her back turned so she couldn't see Pam.

"You really can sing," Nina said. "I

never knew you could sing that well!"

"Neither did I," Emily said with a laugh.

"That's right," Mr. Benson added with a smile. "Sometimes we surprise ourselves when we do things we didn't think we could do. Good job, Emily!"

Pam never did apologize. And she kept trying to upset Emily by making fun of her in front of people. Robert had been right. Bullies don't just disappear. Neither does the hurt. But as the days and weeks went by, a lot of the kids in Emily's class stopped thinking Pam was so funny. Before long, Emily began making some new friends.

One of these friends was Nina. When

Nina decided to sit with Emily and Annie one day at lunch, Pam got mad. She came right over to the table and said in a loud voice, "This must be where all the losers sit!"

Nina looked a little worried at first, but she didn't move. She just ignored Pam and offered Emily and Annie some cookies. When Pam gave Nina's chair a little kick, Nina looked at her and calmly said, "I think you owe my chair an apology."

Some of the kids nearby snickered. An older boy looked at Pam and said, "What's your problem anyway? They're just trying to eat lunch."

After that, Pam stayed at her own table with Jen.

• • •

It was very hard for Emily to lose her best friend. Sometimes, she really missed all the things she and Pam used to do. Now, when she looked at the old picture of the two of them side by side in strollers, it made her very sad. Emily's mother told her that it was okay to feel sad. But she also told her that she was proud of her for standing up for herself. And she said that Emily should feel good about making new friends.

And Emily did feel good. Her new friends all liked each other for who they were. They were careful to never let jokes go too far. Emily didn't have to worry about these friends saying mean things and then saying, "I was just kidding!" She didn't have to worry about them being bullies.

Maybe best friends don't always stay best

friends after all, Emily wrote in her diary near the end of the school year. *But new friends who are true friends are awesome!*